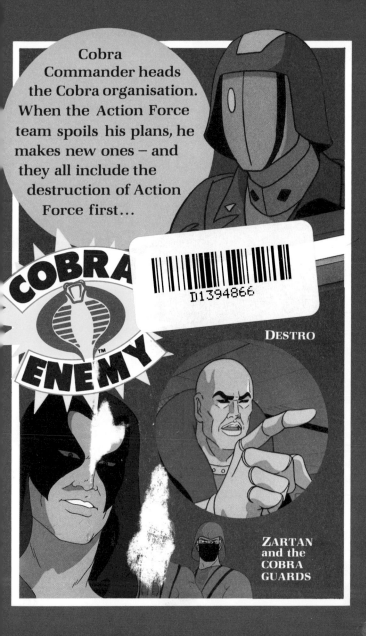

Cobra Commander heads the Cobra organisation. When the Action Force team spoils his plans, he makes new ones – and they all include the destruction of Action Force first…

COBRA ENEMY

D1394866

DESTRO

ZARTAN and the COBRA GUARDS

ACTION FORCE

Action Force is the code name for a highly trained rapid deployment specialist mission force. They are selected from the cream of the world's fighting forces.

ACTION BRIEF

To defend human freedom against Cobra, a ruthless organisation determined to rule the world.

ACTION MISSION

To discover why Cobra forces have kidnapped an entire sleepy village, then to close down the Cobra operation.

Acknowledgment
Co-ordination by Upstart Books Ltd.

British Library Cataloguing in Publication Data
Ware, Christopher J.
    Flint's holiday.—(Action force).
    I. Series
    823'.914[J]   PZ7
    ISBN 0-7214-1061-8

First edition
Published by Ladybird Books Ltd Loughborough Leicestershire UK
Ladybird Books Inc Lewiston Maine 04240 USA
© MCMLXXXVII MILTON BRADLEY INTERNATIONAL INC
© MCMLXXXVII LADYBIRD BOOKS LTD in text and presentation

Printed in England

ACTION ☆ FORCE
INTERNATIONAL HEROES
TM

FLINT'S HOLIDAY

story adaptation by C J Ware

Ladybird Books

The Action Force team are always on stand-by. But even Warrant Officer Flint needs a holiday sometimes. So he decided to pay his cousins a surprise visit at Pleasant Cove. When he arrived, he was worried by their unusually cold greeting.

Flint found the whole family staring at the television, looking exhausted. Within ten minutes of his arrival, they had all gone to bed!

"Oh well, I suppose I might as well go to bed too," he thought.

Next morning, however, he grew even more worried. Flint was up at 6 am as usual – but the whole family had left the house before him.

He knew that his cousins usually got up late.

Frowning, he wandered to the open door. To his amazement he saw streams of neighbours shuffling slowly along the pavement, all with the same glazed look on their faces.

Next moment, the reason was clear. There behind them was one of Action Force's deadliest enemies – a Cobra guard!

This obviously needed checking out. Flint followed the column of neighbours down to Pleasant Cove's port.

There, before his horrified gaze, men, women and children were all climbing into a Cobra submarine.

Then a Cobra guard spotted him, and launched a Full Intruder Alert.

Flint leapt into his car and with a squeal of tyres, raced off through the quiet streets.

But as he hurtled along the coast road, two Cobra helicopters buzzed overhead, aiming their lasers at the car.

Flint reached for his own hand laser, and steering the car with one hand, he took aim and blew an enemy helicopter clean out of the sky.

The remaining Cobra pilot squeezed his firing button as Flint's car eased into his laser sights. The pilot's aim was good. The multi-tron laser reached its mark.

Flint's tyres screeched as flames leapt from the direct hit. The car skidded across the road, smashed through the cliff face barrier and launched out into thin air.

Flint snapped open his seat belt. Then, with a super-human leap, he jumped from the blazing car towards the cliff face. He fell towards the rocks below until the branch of a scrawny tree caught his fall.

Flint gasped as his car plunged into the sea below.

Shaking with strain, he clawed his way back up the cliff only to be met by Zartan, one of Cobra's most ruthless agents.

"Pity about your car," he said, gloating. "And an even bigger pity about you. You're going to be our latest recruit!"

Flint was bundled into a car, then into the Cobra submarine. Minutes later, he found himself in an underwater world, beneath a huge man-made dome on the sea floor.

"Welcome, Flint," said a familiar voice. It was Cobra Commander. "Your cousins and their neighbours are all here, working for me. Watch thisss, my friend," he hissed, turning to a video screen.

At first all Flint saw was a harmless news report. Then his eyes glazed over – he was under Cobra control!

Back at Action Force living quarters, Breaker's television programme was suddenly interrupted.

"Nationsss of the world," hissed Cobra Commander from the screen, "I have a weapon in my Undersea Cccity capable of killing all the earth's land vegetation – like thisss!"

The screen showed a jungle becoming an uninhabitable desert by means of a spectacular explosion!

"Unless I am made your sssupreme leader within eight hoursss, thisss will be your fate!"

"Hey, that's Flint in the background!" said Lady Jaye, watching. "If they've captured Flint, they must be near Pleasant Cove. Alert all forces!"

Shortly, Lady Jaye and Breaker parachuted into Pleasant Cove.

The two Action Force team members made their way up to the satellite dish compound, and immobilised the guards round the empty control room.

Inside they found a relay station transmitting the evening news from a national TV station.

Breaker settled in front of the screen and started to retune the controls.

"Just as I thought!" he said. "Look what happens when I show only every twentieth frame of the news, cutting out the frames in between."

Instantly, the calm TV newsreader disappeared and was replaced by Cobra Commander. His voice hissed instructions to the citizens of Pleasant Cove.

"He's hypnotising the whole town by subliminal suggestion!" exclaimed Breaker.

"What on earth is that?" asked Lady Jaye.

"Cobra Commander is flashing up on one frame in twenty, which is too fast for your eye to see at normal speed. But your brain still adds the frames together and receives a message without you realising," said Breaker.

"Stay here and see if you can do anything to alter the message, while I call up some help," ordered Lady Jaye.

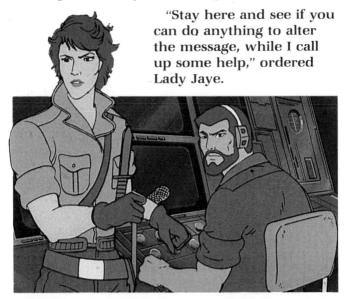

Out in the bay, the Action Force member Shipwreck and the rest of the crew were running into opposition from Cobra Moray's pirates and Cobra's war-loving Baroness.

The Baroness, scenting battle, fired a torpedo into the back of Shipwreck's jet-hover.

Back in harbour, all Cobra forces were watching the fireworks of the sea battle, and Lady Jaye realised her comrades needed support. She slipped past the distracted guards into the Cobra submarine.

Once on board the empty submarine, she used her training to sail out to the battle and rescue Shipwreck, Tripwire and the crew from their burning jet-hover.

"Thanks, Lady Jaye.
It was getting a little
rough," admitted
Shipwreck.

"Now, I need your naval expertise to help to
make it a little rough for Cobra Commander in
his undersea world," replied Lady Jaye. "That
madman's rocket countdown is running out!"

Working together, Shipwreck and Lady Jaye
had no trouble submerging the Cobra
submarine. Using Cobra sea charts and radio
call signs, they sailed it right into the undersea
world, without raising the Cobra alarm.

"When we dock, you search out the rocket,
Tripwire, and we'll see about saving the
Pleasant Cove victims," commanded Lady Jaye.

Cobra Commander spotted the Action Force team climbing out of the submarine. His voice burst from every loudspeaker: "Attention, all workersss. The cccity isss under attack! Repulsssse the intrudersss at all cossstsss! REPEAT, AT ALL COSSSTSSS!"

The hypnotised townsfolk beat feebly at the well trained Action Force members.

"Don't harm them," ordered Lady Jaye.

But, as she spoke, she found herself under attack from the hypnotised Flint! He was the stronger and forced Lady Jaye back into one of the air locks.

Cobra Commander watched the combat with delight. "Flint," he hissed over the loudspeaker. "Flood the air lock."

Flint reached for the flood lever.

"They will be drowned in there," said Cobra's deputy, Destro.

"Yesss, isssn't that deliccciousss?" sneered Cobra Commander.

Meanwhile, Breaker was making progress back at the satellite station, with the help of Bazooka, who had flown in to provide back up.

Bazooka snatched a portrait of Cobra Commander from the satellite station wall and placed it in front of a TV camera. Meanwhile, Breaker broke in on the national network to make his own news announcement.

"Ignore that crazy Cobra Commander! Return to the submarine immediately!"

At once, the victims came out of their trance and flocked towards the waiting submarine.

In Undersea Control, Cobra Commander was still engrossed in the "televised" fight between Flint and Lady Jaye.

But suddenly the fight disappeared from the screen to be replaced by Breaker's "announcement" and Bazooka making faces.

Cobra Commander shouted, "Who isss that fool? How dare he do that! Get him off the screen!"

In a rage, he blasted the TV image with his laser.

As Flint heard Cobra Commander's voice being replaced by Breaker's, the hypnotic spell started to wear off. He relaxed his grip on the air lock control.

His own mind began to take over once more, but he felt dizzy as he came to his senses.

"Where… where are we?" he stuttered.

"Flint, you're back to normal!" cried Lady Jaye. "Come on, there's no time to lose. We have to stop Cobra launching a rocket that will reduce the world to a desert!"

Down in the rocket bay, Tripwire was working.

Carefully, he unscrewed the magnetic bolts.

"It's set to launch in ten minutes," he reported through his headset to Action Force Command. "I've opened the control panel, but this is a tricky one. I could disconnect the launch mechanism, but if I even touch it, the rocket's programmed to launch right now!"

In the undersea world control centre, Cobra Commander boasted to Destro, "Action Forccce are powerlesss to ssstop me! The launch of my beautiful weapon isss only sssecondsss away. Ha, ha…"

Tripwire fled from the rocket bay as the countdown ended, and, with Lady Jaye and Flint, he raced towards Cobra's control room. Flint was first through the door.

"Hold it right there, Cobra Commander!"

"You're too late, Action Force ssscum! The rocket blassstsss off... right... now!" Cobra Commander sneered.

"I wasn't able to de-activate the rocket," said Tripwire.

"Then the world shall pay for your incompetenccce."

"Not really! I re-routed it straight out into space, instead!" said Tripwire, triumphantly.

"What! Well, you may have won thisss battle, but you won't live to tell about it," exclaimed Cobra Commander, as he pressed the undersea world destruct button.

"If we drown, so do you, Cobra!" said Tripwire.

"That'sss what you think, Action Forccce."

Cobra Commander and his henchmen stood their ground for a second, then grinned as their floor section began to lower them out of the stricken control room.

Already, water was pouring into the undersea world onto the Cobra guards.

"Head for the sub," shouted Lady Jaye. "If the water hits the main generator…"

"…we'll be in trouble!" finished Shipwreck, as they reached the submarine.

The hatches clanged shut on the submarine just as the roof of the dome finally caved in, swamping the undersea world.

All round the Cobra submarine, the surging
water hammered at the vessel as Flint steered
out through the wrecked main air lock.

"I hope the submarine survives all this
battering," said Lady Jaye, tensely.

"Do you think Cobra Commander has been
drowned?" asked Shipwreck, as at last the
submarine sped away from the wreckage.

"No, that poisonous villain and his crowd are
bound to have saved their own
skins if nothing
else," said Flint.

Back at Pleasant Cove, Flint took the Action Force team to his cousins' home.

"Do you think Cobra's finished?" asked cousin Ted.

"No, the only thing that's finished is my car – and my holiday!"

"Oh, I forgot to tell you," cut in Lady Jaye, "Colonel Sharp said you could take two more weeks' leave."

"We'd love you to stay, Flint," said Ted.

"Pleasant Cove owes Action Force everything. We'd like you to stay on and see what a real Pleasant Cove welcome is like," said Natalie.

"It's great to see you safe," said Flint. "Thanks all the same though, cousins, but I want to get back on duty where I can get some peace and quiet. These holidays really give me a headache!"

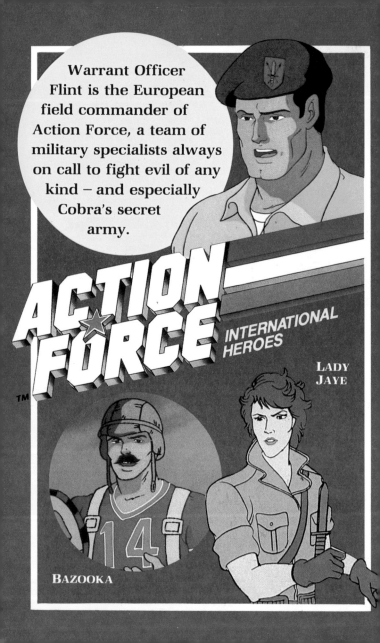